DEVOTED TO WICKED

Devoted Lovers (Book 1.5)

by

Shayla Black

Devoted to Wicked
A Wicked Lovers/Devoted Lovers
Crossover Novella, Book 1.5
Written by Shayla Black

This book is an original publication by Shayla Black.

Copyright © 2017 Shelley Bradley LLC
Print Edition

Cover Design by: Rachel Connolly
Edited by: Amy Knupp of Blue Otter

Excerpt from *Devoted to Pleasure* © 2018 by Shelley Bradley LLC
Excerpt from *More Than Want You* © 2017 by Shelley Bradley LLC
Excerpt from *Wicked Ties* © 2007 by Shelley Bradley LLC

ISBN: 978-1-936596-51-5

ABOUT DEVOTED TO WICKED

A one-night stand…or something more? Karis isn't sure until a thief strands her in Mexico, leaving her in need of a passport photo—and a hero—and giving Cage a second chance to win her love.

This book is a cross-over between both the Wicked Lovers and Devoted Lovers series.

KARIS WESTON PACED the cold tile floor of her hotel room, not really seeing the oceanfront paradise that had lured her to Cancún. It had been twelve hours—a whole night—since she'd sent out a cry for help. She hadn't slept a wink, hadn't stopped shaking, hadn't stopped wondering why someone had targeted *her*.

The phone on the nightstand jangled loudly. She started and gasped, then lunged for the receiver and pressed it to her ear. "Hello?"

"Karis?"

"Yeah." She breathed a sigh of relief at the familiar voice. "Cutter? Thank god. Did Jolie pass you my message? What's going on? I didn't hear from her. Are she and the baby—"

"They're fine. Take a deep breath. Your sister got your message and called me because she and Heath have gone to the hospital to—"

"The hospital?" Alarm pealed through Karis. "So they're not fine? I told Jolie that all those long hours at the office, even if Betti's expansion is going well, was bad for her pregnancy and—"

"Hold up. She's not having a miscarriage. Your mother dropped in unexpectedly after she and Wayne the Pain broke up."

The sarcasm in Cutter's voice mirrored Karis's own opinion. Her mom should never have started dating her soon-to-be ex-husband's brother.

"Is my mom okay?" *Other than not being smart about her love life…*

"Apparently Wayne drove to Dallas early this morning so he could tell Diana face to face that he never had any intention of leaving his wife. Your mom got mad and um…swung a garden hoe at him—don't ask—but caught herself in the leg instead. She's having an x-ray and stitches now." He huffed. "Things are handled here, but Jolie can't come to Mexico, and Heath needs to stay behind to make sure she doesn't overdo it. That's why they called me. Tell me what happened with you, little gypsy."

Karis softened at his nickname for her. Despite getting off to an awkward start, she and Cutter had become fast friends when he'd done his best to bodyguard her through a threat to Jolie and her women's apparel company, Betti. Too bad she couldn't have mustered an iota of chemistry with him. He was a great guy.

Unlike his older brother, Cage, who was a raving jackass.

She knew that…and yet, just like her mother, Karis had let her terrible taste in men tell her hormones that it was a fabulous idea to fall for the older Bryant. In fact, she'd taken one look at him, flashed hot all over, and instantly wondered if he could be her soul mate. After too much tequila and an amazing one-night stand, proof of his assholery had soon cured her of that notion.

If she saw him on her deathbed, it would still be too soon.

"You there?" Cutter prodded. "Did you hear me?"

Focus. "Yeah. Just trying to collect my thoughts. I'm rattled. I haven't slept. I don't feel safe and—"

"You've been through a lot. I'm tied up here in Dallas but don't worry. I sent the cavalry. He should arrive any moment. You're going to be all right."

She froze. "Who did you send?"

A pounding on the door interrupted the conversation, startling Karis. She pressed a hand to her chest.

"That's him now," Cutter said. "You two can call me later."

Oh, he better *not* have done what she suspected, not if he wanted to keep his balls. "Who did you freaking send?"

Cutter didn't answer right away. "Relax. You're in good hands. I'll hold down the fort here. I'm sure your sister will update you about your mom when she has news. See you when you get home, little gypsy. Take care."

"Don't you even think—"

But Cutter did more than think about hanging up. She'd only finished half her sentence when he actually did. Damn it. Grumbling, she slammed the phone down.

Maybe she was wrong. Maybe Cage wasn't on the other side of the door, waiting to needle and poke and irritate her with his disreputable good looks and signature tomcat smile. But when she stomped across the room and wrenched the door open, all her wishful thinking went out the window.

"Hi, cupcake." He gave her a wink and a teasing smile.

She knew exactly what sort of man he was and yet he still made her belly flutter. *What is wrong with me?*

The muss of his golden hair hung low on his forehead, flirting with his eyes. He clearly hadn't shaved in a couple of days, and the stubble dusting his jaw made it look even sharper. He'd abandoned his winter coat and draped it over the duffel dangling from his right hand in favor of a faded blue tank top that read TEQUILA AND TACOS.

Karis gritted her teeth and did her best to ignore the broad, bulging muscles of his shoulders, now filling her doorframe. She didn't like Cage here because she didn't like him, period. She didn't want to *feel* anything for him. Been there, done that. She'd burned the T-shirt. He was the kind of man who would never be faithful. After a lifetime of watching her mother fall for that kind of guy repeatedly only to wind up brokenhearted every time, she refused to follow suit.

Sure, she could slam the door in his face or play dumb and ask why he'd come. But her sister and brother-in-law couldn't help her out of this scrape. Neither could Cutter. She'd already tried to solve her problem alone, to no avail. If she wanted to go home, she had to rely on Cage. Spend time with him. Talk to him. No doubt she would have to resist him, too.

She sighed. "Come in."

Cage strolled inside her hotel room, his tall, rangy body crowding her against the doorway. He peered at her with dark, hungry eyes as he dropped his bag. "You look good."

She glanced down at herself. Her entire vacation wardrobe had consisted of bikinis, cover-ups, an occasional pair of short-shorts, and high-heeled sandals. This morning after tossing and turning sleeplessly, she'd rushed through a shower, wondering if whoever had scared the hell out of her intended to come back and finish the job. Absently, she'd tossed on an off-white, almost-too-small bikini with a rose-and-swirl pattern over her breasts. The contraption was held together by thin, sunny yellow straps. Cage's stare walked all over her top before straying to the lone flower barely covering her down there. Sure, she'd tossed on a lacy cover-up but it was entirely transparent, there for decoration more than actual protection from the sun or prying eyes.

If she'd known she was going to have to deal with Cage, she would have brought turtlenecks and mom jeans or a nun's habit—something to ensure he'd never look at her twice.

Refusing to let his perusal fluster her more, Karis shut the door behind him with a soft snick. This wasn't about them or the night they'd spent together, just about ending this ill-advised vacation and getting home.

"You mean I look good for a girl who's had everything important stolen from her hotel room and currently has no way of getting home? Don't bother with the compliment. I don't need it."

Her reply came out bitchier than she intended. It had been a rough night, and she was always grouchy when she hadn't slept. Coupled with all the uncertainty, the hint of danger, and the feeling that she'd been violated, Karis wasn't at her best.

"You need help." Cage's face softened. "I understand and I'll help you. But just saying…you always look good to me."

The unexpected compliment came out both sincere and serious—two things she would never have imagined Cage was capable of. She tried not to let his words make her feel marshmallowy inside.

"Thanks." She gave a halfhearted shrug. "I'm sorry your brother sent you to 'rescue' me. I know you have better things to do."

"I don't."

She frowned. "This is awkward."

"Not for me."

Of course not. Everything seemed to roll off his back, even the feelings she'd shared with him that breathtaking night. Whatever. It wasn't as if she cared. Okay, she did…a little. But he didn't need to know that. The best way to convey ambivalence was to simply pretend that he didn't affect her one way or another.

"Great. I appreciate you coming here to help me out. Did your brother have you bring my passport photo so I can get home?"

"Yeah." He made no move to hand it over. "But you still haven't told me what happened."

She sighed. For whatever reason, he wasn't going to just hand over the picture. Did he think that after what happened a few weeks ago she'd be amenable to falling into bed with him once more?

Think again, buster.

"I've been on this vacation with Jolie's receptionist and my friend, Wisteria. She just broke up with her boyfriend." Again, but this time most likely for good. "I came back to the room after dinner and a couple of drinks at the pool bar. The door was wide open. Someone had picked the lock on my suitcase and taken everything—cash, what little jewelry I have, credit card, and my passport. I told Wisteria to go home on the flight we'd originally booked this morning. No sense in her losing a plane ticket and missing work when she couldn't help me. Then I called my sister, who called Cutter, who apparently called you. That's it."

He nodded. "Anybody following you while you've been here?"

Now he was slipping into cop mode. It was his job, and she was glad he had skills, but it probably wasn't going to help this far from Dallas. "Not that I'm aware of."

He scowled. "Anybody been flirting with you?"

Karis refused to answer that question. She'd come here in part to escape the sudden cold that had enveloped the North Texas area as January came to a close…and in part to forget Cage. They'd spent one hell of a New Year's Eve together, and with every kiss and touch, she'd believed they had something special. What she'd discovered the following week had blown that foolish hope to hell.

She lifted her shoulder in an offhanded shrug. "It's not as if I came here to be alone."

Karis hadn't planned to be…but she had somehow ended up by herself. On their first night here, Wisteria had met a hunk from the Hill Country, located a couple of hours south of Dallas. The two of them had hit it off instantly. Hayden seemed completely different from her previous douche of a boyfriend, and they had been inseparable for the seven days and six nights they'd vacationed in Cancún. In truth, she'd barely seen Wisteria after the woman had met him. And as luck would have it, he'd been able to change his flight to travel home with her. She was probably landing in Dallas now and finding something way more interesting to do than dealing with the former lover she wished she'd never taken.

Cage's jaw clenched. "Who have you been spending time with while you've been here?"

He sounded a little bit jealous.

"I'm sure it hardly matters, especially to you."

"Is that what you think?" He cocked his head and sent her a challenging stare. "Enlighten me why."

She had this fantasy of telling him she'd figured out he was a cheater and a liar, but what would it solve? She refused to give him the satisfaction or to care what he did anymore. And if she kept her attitude nonchalant, he would back off sooner or later.

She shrugged. "Well, the night we spent together was pretty meaningless, so—"

"Is that how you'd categorize it?"

Now he sounded downright pissed, so she switched tactics. "Can we talk about that later? Right now, I'd really like to focus on getting my paperwork in order so I can go home. Isn't that the reason you're here?"

He didn't look pleased, and Karis wondered why he wasn't breathing a sigh of relief that she'd let him off the proverbial hook.

"All right," he said finally. "Have you talked to resort security? The *policía*?"

"Yeah. Apparently, there are no security cameras in the hallways, so they can only see people coming off and getting on the elevators, but I was gone during a three-hour window and a lot of people were milling around my floor during that time. So I don't expect anything will come from the police report. I spent part of last night printing out the forms on the State Department's website so I can get a new passport. Thankfully, I still had my driver's license in my pocket, so all I needed was the passport picture. Thanks for bringing it to me. FedEx would have worked, too. But I can take it from here."

"Look at you go, Miss Independent," he quipped, shaking his head. "But that's not how this works. I'll be staying with you until you fly home."

She gaped at him. "It will probably be a couple of days."

"All right."

A terrible thought occurred to her. "Where do you think you're sleeping?"

With a glance around, he took in the room—the unforgiving tile floors, the sofa that was way too short to accommodate his six-three frame, and the king-size bed. He nodded at the mattress. "Next to you. It's not as if we haven't slept together before."

Karis stepped back. It was one thing to resist him for a couple of hours, but he looked good enough to nibble, eat, slurp, suck, and lick. How would she outlast him for a couple of days? Her willpower wasn't that strong, especially because she remembered how mind-blowing he was in the sack.

"No. Absolutely not." She shook her head.

"Your sister made me promise I'd stay with you, get to the bottom of this, and escort you safely to your plane. I'm a man who keeps his word."

She almost snorted at that, but he hadn't actually made her any promises when they'd rung in the new year together buzzed and naked and orgasmic.

With a sigh, she slung her fist on her hip. It was on the tip of her tongue to ask him what the hell he was up to, but she refused to get into this now. She simply wanted to go home.

"Can't you get another room?"

"If this thief broke in once, what's to say he couldn't do it again?" Cage glanced back at the door. "I don't see any sign of forced entry. And since they don't have electronic key cards, I'm guessing he picked the lock with a little finesse. What's to stop him from coming back for seconds?"

Nothing. Which was why Karis hadn't slept a wink last night. "Fine. You can sleep here. Keep your hands and any other roving parts of your body to yourself."

He shrugged and flipped her the kind of annoying half smile that made her want to scream and climb his body all at once. "We'll see, cupcake."

AFTER DICKING AROUND at the US Embassy for most of the day and getting Karis's paperwork in order, Cage helped her into a taxi and they headed back to the resort. The officials said they would do their best to process her passport in two business days. He was hopeful that would happen, but he wasn't holding his breath.

Once they'd reached the upscale land of palm trees, umbrella drinks, and crystal water, Cage all but carried Karis up to her room. By the time they got through the door, she looked ready to fall over.

"Take a nap. I'll order us some room service."

She shook her head. "I'm going to find a lounger by the pool and some food. You can stay and nap if you want."

A biting quip streaked through his brain, but he swallowed it back. Not for the first time, he wondered what was up her ass. Their New Year's fling had been everything. Ground-shaking.

Life-altering. Heart-bending. The next morning, he'd gotten tied up in an unforeseeable situation that had taken a long, sad week to extricate himself from. He'd called Karis the moment he could. She'd wanted absolutely nothing to do with him then—or now. Even repeated calls to his brother hadn't shed any light.

"Wherever you go, I'm going, too."

She looked exasperated but too exhausted to argue. "Suit yourself."

He almost told her that he always did—then she started peeling off her T-shirt and shimmying out of her shorts to reveal the tiny bikini beneath. Yeah, he'd seen it through the short, lacy getup she'd been wearing earlier, but now there was absolutely nothing to disrupt his view of her lean, sun-kissed body. The top barely contained her lush breasts. He didn't mind seeing her cleavage and healthy swells at all…but he didn't want some other guy looking at them.

As she reached for a cover-up and a pair of flip-flops, he grabbed the room key and thrust it in his pocket. "Lead the way."

When he opened the door, she sidled past him, looking over her shoulder. "You don't have to babysit me."

Cage let the door shut and checked the lock behind him. Flimsier than shit. Theft was likely a raging problem here if that was the best defense between the contents of a guest's room and a stranger.

Shaking his head, he hustled to catch up to Karis, who was halfway down the hall, pretty ass swishing with every step. Fuck, he hadn't forgotten brushing the underwear from those cheeks, kissing them during his oral travels across her body, clutching them as he plunged deeper into her with every thrust.

"You been wearing that bathing suit around the resort all week?" He glanced at the round flesh half peeking out from the formfitting fabric.

Her thighs looked sleek, as if she was the sort of girl whose cardio often included a good run. She had a bit of thigh gap, enough to look good in tiny outfits but not so much that he worried she was starving. Her filigree tattoo began mid-back and wound gracefully to the small of her spine with feminine swirls and curved lines, then disappeared into her bikini bottoms. It turned him the fuck on. Everything about her did, from the wispy ringlets curling at her nape in the humidity to her narrow feet.

"I've got a collection of similar ones. Why?" She pressed the button to call the elevator.

Because he was hard-pressed to believe that men at this resort hadn't been tripping all over themselves to get close to her. Instead, it looked as if someone had chosen to take the goodies in her suitcase rather than the goodies in her panties. To him, that didn't make sense.

As the elevator doors opened with a ding, she stepped inside and he followed. "I'm wondering if you might have flirted with or rebuffed someone around here who decided to get your attention in a totally different way."

"I've talked to a lot of people."

Cage didn't want to imagine who.

When it came to one-night stands, Karis was hardly his first rodeo. He had no idea why he was so hung up…except that there was something about her. She'd felt better than good in his arms. She'd been funny and sensitive, sexy and interesting. Different. Vulnerable.

He'd never been that guy who lost his head over a woman. Hell, he'd barely had a romantic relationship that lasted more than a few weeks. One-nighters and friends with benefits were more his speed. But he'd hoped Karis took him more seriously, wanted more from him than sex.

Now, Cage was beginning to think he'd been a dumb ass and that she'd just wanted a good lay after all. It sucked. "Stop dancing around my questions and tell me the truth. Have you slept with anyone since you've been here?"

She reared back at him. "Not that it's any of your business—"

"Well, if you want me to help keep you safe until your paperwork comes through, then I have to figure out who might have gone stalker on you."

"It was a theft," she reminded as the elevator descended.

"Absolutely, but he didn't take anything of Wisteria's?"

Her frown said that puzzled her, too. "No."

"I noticed your iPad was still on your nightstand, so he didn't take that, either. How much was your jewelry worth?"

"Next to nothing."

"How much cash did you have?"

"Forty bucks I stuck back in case of an emergency. The rest of it was in my pocket."

"And has he tried to use your credit cards?"

She paused, then shook her head. "So far, no." And she sounded almost puzzled by that. "When I called to cancel them, the banks said there'd been no activity on the accounts at all."

He nodded. "Normally, that's the first thing a thief would use because they know the numbers will be voided soon. So mostly what this guy took from you was your way out of the country."

The elevator came to a shaking stop. After a long moment, the doors opened. Automatically, Cage fitted a hand at the small of Karis's back and escorted her out. She shivered at his touch. He couldn't miss it, just like he couldn't escape the zip of heat that flooded his blood and settled into his cock.

With a little jerk, she pulled away and looked back at him with a warning not to lay hands on her again.

What the hell? The night they'd met, she hadn't been able to get naked with him fast enough. She hadn't been able to pull him inside her deep enough. She hadn't been able to slake her hunger often enough. In fairness, he hadn't either. From the moment his younger brother had introduced them, she'd reduced him into a puddle of oil, then tossed her flames all over him. The bonfire they generated had been a fucking combustible conflagration.

Now she seemed to have the personality of a glitchy freezer.

"Maybe...you're right," she conceded. "I didn't stop to look at the situation that way."

"You were too rattled. You felt violated."

"Yeah." The glance she gave Cage as she made her way to the pool bar said she was more than surprised he understood.

"And you're mad, too."

"Totally."

She looked even more shocked at his insight. Really, it wasn't that hard to guess. He heard from victims every day on the beat. But it was nice to have found a point of connection with her. Still, it didn't stop him from needing some facts. "So let's try this again. Have you slept with anyone since you've been here? He'll be my first suspect."

"No."

Cage held in his sigh of relief. He didn't have the right to expect that he was the only man in her life—yet. But he couldn't deny that he wanted to be. "Anyone who...I don't know, bought you a drink?"

"It's an all-inclusive resort. The booze is included."

"Or any gesture like that. Someone who shared a meal with you? Invited you to his room?"

"No." She tossed on her sunglasses as they emerged from the brightly colored lobby to the infinity edge pool overlooking the Caribbean Sea.

At the restaurant's entrance, they waited for someone to seat them. A few moments later, a smiling young, dark-eyed woman showed them to a table on the waterfront, tucked under the shade provided by the grassy roof overhead, swaying slightly in the warm tropical wind.

He helped Karis into her chair, then they both grabbed a menu from the table as the sun began to sink to the west. They both did a quick scan before setting the laminated list of foods aside. The moment they did, a Hispanic waiter approached the table with two glasses of water in hand—and eyes only for Karis.

"Hello, señorita. *Buenas noches.* How have you been?" He smiled as he set the water down, a glass in front of each plate.

"I'm all right. Thanks, Miguel."

The twenty-something punk—probably closer to Karis's age—beamed. "Thank you for remembering me, Señorita Karis. You look *muy bonita.*"

When he winked, Cage wanted to hurl. How often did the guy use that line on lonely tourists? He was good-looking enough, so it probably worked more often than it should.

It wouldn't have any impact on Karis, Cage decided. Not while he was here.

"I appreciate that." She gave him a small, slightly dismissive smile, obviously ready to order.

"Were you not supposed to travel home this morning?" Miguel asked.

She nodded, looking glum and agitated. "Yeah. Someone stole my passport last night, so I'll be here another couple of days."

The waiter turned a shocked expression her way. To Cage, it looked awfully staged.

"That is terrible. I'm so sorry someone would mar the Mexican hospitality we have done our best to show you this week with an act so callous. If I can do anything beyond bring you food to be of assistance—"

"I'll take care of her," Cage assured.

The slick Latin lover finally looked at him, expression tightening. "Señor. Hello. Are you a new guest with us, then?"

"Looks like it."

His mouth pursed further as he slid another stolen glance at Karis. No doubt, the little shit was displeased.

"Very good," Miguel said as if having him here were anything but, then turned his attention back to Karis. "What may I bring you today?"

She leaned her elbows on the table, probably not realizing how much cleavage she flashed the waiter. "I'll take a chicken quesadilla and a margarita, heavy on the tequila, light on the salt."

"For you, señorita *bonita*, anything." He clapped a hand to his heart, then flung his arms out to her as if to say he was giving her all his love.

Cage resisted the urge to puke—or throw a punch. Instead, he settled for taking Karis's hand across the table and holding it firmly when she—predictably—tried to pull away. "I'll have the same. And some privacy to talk to my girlfriend."

At his words, Miguel scowled before masking it with a politely bland expression. "Of course. Let me know if you would like anything else."

Then the waiter finally melted away.

"Your girlfriend?" Karis hissed the moment Miguel disappeared from earshot, pulling her hand free. "Let's get one thing straight—"

"We're going to get a lot of things straight," Cage assured her. "But I can almost guarantee he's your suspect."

"What? He's just a guy I ordered meals from this week."

"He knows your name."

"He knew Wisteria's name, too. Being friendly is part of his job."

He snorted. "The guy wasn't so friendly with me."

"Miguel just met you."

"Still, I guarantee he's never going to call me señorita *bonita*."

She stared at him across the table as if he'd lost his mind. Hell, maybe he had. Karis Weston did something to him. He didn't want to argue with her. He just wanted to get deep inside her and stay.

"I thought you'd be happy he didn't call you a pretty lady. But hey, if you want him to, maybe you have a whole private life I don't know anything about."

Cage gritted his teeth. That was it. He was determined to get to the bottom of whatever was eating at her. Sure, she was thrown off by the theft and the abrupt change of her plans. She'd probably wanted the comfort of her sister, not the guy she'd fucked once, then rebuffed. And if she itched to take her frustration out on him, he could deal with that. But her hostility seemed to stem from a different place. He had to understand it if he was going to call a truce and move them past it.

With a deep breath, Cage looked her way. "My point is, Miguel knew your name and when you were leaving. He's a terrible actor, and I don't believe for one second that he was shocked someone had stolen your stuff. Since the moment he opened his mouth, my instincts have been screaming. I think he's your bad guy."

Finally, Karis looked as if she was considering his words. "That would make him a little unhinged. I mean, we've talked some, sure. Wisteria, Hayden, Miguel, another waiter, and I closed down the bar one night and had a ball. But nothing happened between us. I didn't give him any reason to think we were a 'thing,' even temporarily."

"Some guys have been known to assume more intimacy with less encouragement. I'll keep investigating, but I'm just saying...I've got a bad feeling about him."

Karis cocked her head and leaned her elbows on the table. "I can't tell whether you're for real or just being stupidly jealous."

"Both." Why lie?

A little frown settled between her brows, like his assertion confused her. "Wow. That may be the first honest thing you've ever said to me."

What? "I haven't lied to you once, cupcake. I didn't lie to you when we met or when I told you that night I wanted you or when I said the next morning I wasn't sure I'd ever get enough of you."

She dipped her head to cover the flush that rushed up her cheeks. "You're right. But I didn't realize what a player you are. Don't worry, I got the message quick."

Now, he was getting to the crux of her nose being out of joint. "What message was that?"

"New Year's didn't mean anything, and you already had someone in your life." She leaned back in her chair and glanced out at the ocean, as if she couldn't bear to look at him.

As if he'd hurt her.

He mulled that for a minute, along with her words. "I don't have an exclusive relationship with anyone. I never have."

Karis flinched, then tried to shrug off her reaction as if it meant nothing. "So it's normal for you to go from one bed to another. Okay. It's your life."

Suddenly, Cage suspected he knew exactly what had happened. "Look at me, cupcake."

She rolled her eyes and sighed, but she reluctantly complied. "What?"

He wished he could see behind her sunglasses. He had a feeling there was a wealth of info welling in her eyes, along with some tears, too.

Before he could say another word, Miguel dropped off two huge frozen margaritas and two quesadillas, piled high with sour cream and guacamole. He lingered, offering more napkins and fresh pico de gallo and whatever else he could think of until Cage shooed him away.

"You saw me with a blonde shortly after the night we spent together, didn't you?" he challenged the moment the pesky waiter disappeared.

Karis reared back like she was stunned he'd guessed right. Then she schooled her expression and dug into her plate. "Yeah, but like I said, it's your life. Your brother told me you're not into relationships. It's my fault for not listening and—"

"I wasn't into relationships until you. And that's not a line." He raked a hand through his hair, wondering if there was any way to tell her what he was thinking without revealing all the raw places inside him. But he wasn't good at head games. "This is as straight up as I can be: I've had a lot of friends with benefits. They were pretty much the only female friends I had. But the night I spent with you changed something for me I still don't understand and I don't know how to explain. I'm not sharing benefits with anyone right now because I can't stop thinking about you. I can't stop wanting you. And I'm guessing that somehow you saw me with Madison, the blonde, after the night you and I spent together."

"Yes." Her answer sounded curt and crisp.

She was hurt. Cage understood, and he was relieved to finally have the mystery solved.

"Madison called me literally two minutes after I left your house. We've been friends…" He paused and realized there was no point in being less than honest. "Yes, with benefits, since our senior year of high school."

"You've had her at the top of your booty call speed dial list for the last...what, fifteen years? Clearly, you've tapped that a lot."

He tried not to get pissed off that she wanted to cast the worst possible light on his admission. The last twenty-four hours had not been kind to her. And if he'd seen her cozy up to another man right after their amazing night together, he'd be fucking furious and not very gracious about it, either. Besides, she had daddy issues—just like he did. So he had to cut her some slack.

"Yep. Not even going to deny it. We both treated it casually. She's a career woman who doesn't have time for guys and relationships, but she still sometimes wants a man to hold her. Until I got together with you, I didn't see the difference between screwing and making something more meaningful, so Madison and I never turned one another down. That's the unvarnished truth. But the morning I left you, she called to tell me that she'd just rushed her father to the hospital. She's an only child. Her mother died a few years ago. She was all alone, and she couldn't face what was happening without a shoulder to lean on."

"Oh." Karis stared at him with pursed-mouthed contrition before she took a sip of her drink. "So...you stayed with her while he recovered?"

"Yes and no. He died the next day, so I couldn't just leave her. That's the thing about my friendship. It wasn't simply about the benefits. I tried to be truly supportive, lend her my strength until she could bury her dad almost a week later." When Karis chewed on her lip, mulling his words over, he chowed down on a bite of his meal and took another approach. "What would you think of a man who walked out on a person whose last parent was dying?"

She sighed. "You had to stay. I didn't realize... And now I feel really stupid. I came by to bring you cookies, you know. I barely know how to bake, but for you I tried. Yes, I was that gaga about you. So when I saw you with her on your porch, hugging her and kissing her forehead, I assumed…"

"I would have assumed the same thing, cupcake, if the shoe was on the other foot. I would have been mightily pissed off, too. But I swear, Madison and I haven't exchanged benefits since I've been with you."

"It was a traumatic time for her, and sex was probably the last thing on her mind—"

"Well…" He rubbed at the back of his neck, deciding if he was going to be honest, he better be brutally so. "Actually, she…um, hit me up after the funeral. She needed to feel alive, she said. She needed to forget." He shrugged. "Straight up? I got her off with my fingers so she'd have some relief. I ended it there. Hell, she cried the whole time. But the truth is, after you, I didn't want her sexually anymore."

He glanced Karis's way to gauge her reaction, but she looked blank and unreadable. "Then what happened?"

"Well, I told her that I could no longer be *that* guy for her but I'd always be her friend. *Just* her friend. She was disappointed but she understood. Then I set about trying to open the conversation with you again. You put me off for weeks. And no matter how much I begged, my brother wouldn't help. Then you left for vacation. Here we are."

"Do you have any more friends with benefits I should know about?"

"None I won't think twice about ignoring. I'll even delete them from my phone while you watch, if you want. I'm serious."

"Why do you think what you do matters to me?" She tried to appear unaffected, but he saw her uncertainty.

"Cutter told me about your mom, about all the selfish douches who have cheated and strayed and abandoned your family. My dad was the same kind of asshole, so I know how hard coping with that as a kid can be. It sucks to look up one day to find your dad gone."

Karis bit her lip, and behind her sunglasses he could see her emotion. He was getting to her. Reaching her. He didn't know precisely where they were going, but his every instinct as a cop and as a man told him that nothing right now in his life was more vital than winning this woman back.

"It changes you. I was a kid when my dad walked out. Apparently, he had a girlfriend, and one day he decided that being with her was more important than staying with his wife and daughter. I don't think I ever really forgave him. And it definitely changed the way I approached men and relationships. I was always looking for the guy who wouldn't do that to me." She laughed at herself. "I was looking for Prince Charming."

"And I didn't seem like him."

"That night, I believed you were. I really hoped that you were the guy for me, the faithful one my mother never has found. When Jolie got lucky and fell for Heath, I started letting myself believe it was possible for me, too. Then you felt so…I don't know, right is probably the best word. Like we fit together or something. Like we belonged, you know? Or maybe you don't and I'm just babbling."

"No, I get you totally. I was feeling it, too. So when I was sure Madison wasn't going to fall apart anymore and she understood our relationship now, I called you. When you didn't want to talk to me, I won't lie. I was kinda devastated. But I wasn't going to give up. I'm still not. That's why I'm here."

Karis tucked away another forkful of her quesadilla and washed it back with a sip of her drink. "I have to admit, I'm shocked. I didn't see myself ever being this close to you again."

"How did us being apart make you feel?"

"Crappy. Sad." She hesitated, then finally tore off her sunglasses, revealing the tears pooling in her eyes, just about to spill over the rims. "It hurt."

"Me, too. And that's not bullshit. I don't have any experience with making a woman happy out of bed, but I want to try, see where we could take this."

A pretty little smile crept up her face, which she promptly hid behind her napkin as she wiped her mouth. "All right. I'd like that."

"Me, too. Still hungry?" He nodded at her plate.

"Not really. What about you? You've only eaten two bites."

"Fuck food. I'd rather be with you."

She gulped back the last of her half-melted margarita and left her barely touched plate. "Me, too."

As they rose, Cage caught Miguel staring. He narrowed his eyes at the smooth waiter when his prying glance followed Karis retreating.

The guy approached him, adjusting the jacket of his starched uniform. "Would you like your food to go? I will be happy to find you a box so you can have your meal later."

He didn't like Cage any more than Cage liked the waiter, so the sudden desire to be helpful only made him wonder if Miguel had tainted or poisoned his food. The guy was definitely up to something. "No. But here's what you can do for me: back away from Karis. She's not available. I'm pretty sure you know something about the theft of her passport, and I'm telling you now that I'm here for—and with—her. She doesn't need your 'help' and she never will. Fucking get lost."

Miguel pressed his lips together, seeming to hold in his temper. Cage almost heard the gnashing of his teeth, but the guy collected himself, as if suddenly remembering that he was supposed to deny the accusation. "I stole nothing. I would never do such a thing. I was not aware that attempting to be helpful and friendly would be misconstrued as flirting. Of course I respect our guests' lives and privacy."

Every word Miguel said sounded like a preplanned speech, and Cage wanted to call bullshit. But Karis was waiting at the sliding double doors heading back into the lobby. As much as he'd like to have it out with the waiter until the guy understood that he needed to fuck off, he would ten times rather be with Karis, kissing her, peeling off her clothes, whispering in her ear, making her feel good. Convincing her that he cared about her more than he probably should after one night—and he didn't see that changing anytime soon.

"Great," he growled. "Stay away."

Cage didn't wait around for Miguel's reaction. He also wouldn't underestimate the guy. He'd be willing to bet Karis wasn't the first guest to have her passport and other goodies stolen from her room. He'd also bet the majority of those guests had ended up warming Miguel's bed for a few days.

Racing over to Karis, he hustled her inside the air-conditioned common area, away from the watchful waiter's prying eyes, and took her hand in his. "Can you wait for me by that fountain for two minutes, cupcake?"

She turned to look behind her at the big stone water feature in the middle of the lobby. As evening descended, the place wasn't bursting with people, but enough straggled in with suitcases or hung out with drinks that Cage didn't worry Miguel or some other potential cohort of his could take their anger out on Karis.

"Sure." She looked a little confused but hung back like he'd asked.

He couldn't let her go that simply. Cage gave a gentle tug on her wrist and pulled her against him. After a little sway, her chest collided with his. Her head automatically fell back and she delved into his eyes. Jesus, what was it about her? She was a bit zany, not terribly practical. According to Cutter, she had a free spirit and a gypsy heart. She was his polar opposite.

Maybe that was the attraction. Maybe that was the reason every moment he'd spent with her over New Year's, he'd felt more balanced and more certain that she belonged to him.

Cage didn't dare kiss her now. They might not make it upstairs before his need to feel her again overwhelmed him. Instead, he nuzzled her cheek and pressed his mouth to her ear. "Want to know why I call you cupcake?"

"I've always wondered," she breathed.

"Because from the moment we met, the first thing I thought was how adorable and sweet you were. And just like a cupcake, I could hardly wait to eat you."

He smiled as he left her standing there, looking somewhere between stunned and excited, as he fished his phone from his back pocket and strode across the lobby. Glad he'd picked up an international calling plan before he'd left home, he made his way to the hotel's offices and hit one of the names on his speed dial.

Forest, better known as Trees, was the quietest member of the operative team at EM Security Management, his brother's employer. In fact, Trees was downright scary. All those guys who worked for Hunter and Logan Edgington and Joaquin Muñoz were. All former special operatives, they lived on the edge and craved adrenaline as their drug of choice.

The private security route was all well and good, he supposed. Cutter made good money, and Cage wouldn't sneeze at it, but all he'd ever known was being a cop. It worked for him. These dudes, like Trees, possessed specialized skills that would come in really fucking handy about now.

"Cage?" He sounded surprised.

They didn't talk much and they weren't pals exactly. But they also weren't enemies, so he was hoping the shaved-headed fucker would do him a favor.

"Yeah, look… My girlfriend is down in Mexico…" He filled the guy in on the crap Karis had gone through and whom he suspected was the culprit. "Would you do me a favor and hack into the hotel's employment records, tell me if any of the previous female guests have filed complaints against this guy?"

"On it. Has this Miguel cat threatened her? Do you need backup? Mexico sounds nice. It's really damn cold here, and I can't stand the kind of sniveling asswipe who threatens a woman."

He'd probably offered his assistance more for the vacation than anything, but it was nice all the same.

"I've got it so far, but I'll holler if that changes."

"Roger that."

In the background, Cage heard the guy tapping on a computer at what sounded like lightning speed. He didn't ask how Trees had learned his hacking skills, he just knew from hearing his brother talk that they were mad. He was also both surveillance and navigation on the team. Cutter was in charge of engineering and demolitions, which seemed like an oxymoron to him, so he teased his brother about building something only to blow it up. Josiah and Zyron he didn't know much about. And One-Mile…whatever his current situation with Brea, the guy had still taken advantage of her. In Cage's book, he always be a prick and a half.

But Cage had his own problems right now.

"Can you call me back when you've got something?"

"Yep. They've got some security on this system, and there's the translation problem, but it should only be a couple of hours."

"Thanks, Trees. I owe you big."

"Maybe you can make your brother introduce me to some women in this godforsaken town. I just moved to Lafayette. All the good ones seem to be taken, and my dick is damn tired of my hand."

Cage laughed. "I'll twist my little brother's arm, and we'll work something out."

They ended the call, then Cage strolled to the front desk and asked for the manager. After some backing and forthing, along with a good, old-fashioned bribe, the suit blabbed that Miguel's shift ended in another three hours. Good to know when the pouty little bitch would have free time to make mayhem. He was coming for Karis, no doubt. Cage was determined to be waiting.

STILL STANDING AT the fountain, Karis watched Cage stroll back toward her. What the hell was he up to? It was something, given that swagger. He thought he had everything under control. He'd taken charge of the situation because he was the man and he intended to protect her.

It was actually kind of sweet.

"Hey," she murmured as he approached.

He winked. "You ready to head upstairs?"

Though her heart was pounding, she raised a brow at him. "For a rousing game of Charades?"

"That what you want?"

She wrinkled her nose. "Putting this back on me? Okay, I'll be brave. Not really."

"Good." He pulled her close, and she melted against him. "I promise, I won't leave you guessing what I want."

When he all but yanked her toward the elevator, Karis had to suppress a laugh. She felt lighter than she had in…well, since the start of the new year.

She'd begun January first full of hope and lightness—and impatience for Cage to call again. Seeing him with Madison a few days later had been the worst shock. Wondering if only she had felt the earth move between them had filled Karis with pain. After his explanation today, she understood where he'd been coming from. No, she didn't like that he'd touched the blonde again, but weirdly she understood his act of compassion. People wanted comfort in times of loss. Besides, she and Cage hadn't made each other any promises of exclusivity during their one night together.

Sure, he could be lying about the whole thing. Men did that. But Cage was so much like his true-blue brother that Karis didn't think so.

She pressed the call button. "Jolie could have simply overnighted the picture to me, you know."

He shook his head, the mussed tousle of his hair so sexy. "I was with Cutter when Jolie called him for help. My brother was actually going to come to your rescue." Cage grimaced. "I insisted on coming instead. I never told him what happened between us that night…but he's a smart guy. After he warned me that I'd better bring you back in one piece and not to break your heart, he helped me book the next flight out."

Cage had come for her, seemingly to make things right between them. Karis couldn't think of a single time a man had gone so far out of his way simply to make her life better, keep her safe, or give her a reason to smile.

She slanted him a glance, feeling as if she glowed from within—like her happiness. "Thanks."

The elevator opened with a ding. A family stepped out. She and Cage eased in, totally alone.

"Did you miss me?" he asked as they started to ascend. "Because I missed you like hell."

Once given, Karis knew she couldn't take her answer back. She would be exposing her heart. "I thought about you a lot."

"Ditto, cupcake."

He grabbed her hand as the elevator stopped at their floor. Together, they raced to her room. She felt excitement dancing between them. It gripped her stomach. The ache between her legs swelled.

As he inserted the key in the lock, he studied her. "You need anything? Another drink? A shower? A minute to enjoy the sunset?"

She frowned. Was he trying to distract her because he didn't want to have sex with her after all? "No."

"Thank god." He shoved the portal open, nudged her into the room, then slammed the door and locked it behind him.

Karis barely had time to draw in a breath before he urged her back against the wall, covered her body with his own, and slanted his mouth over her lips in a possessive, toe-curling kiss.

Instantly, she looped her arms around his neck and whimpered. She'd missed him so much. That familiar feeling of belonging to him swamped her again, along with desire. He tasted of tequila, just like he had that first night, as well as something spicy and manly. Cage overwhelmed her senses. He fried her resistance.

She loved it.

He tugged at her pool cover-up, and Karis helped him, breaking the kiss only long enough to whip it over her head. He tossed the garment away and attacked the strings of her bikini next. Between one breath and the next, he exposed her breasts, cupping them, dipping down to lick them, suckle their tips one at a time, then sink lower still to yank down her bikini bottoms.

"Step out. I want your pussy. I've been craving my cupcake something fierce."

Her heart fluttered and her ache coiled as he dragged the scrap of fabric down her thighs. She was still stepping out of them when he lifted one of her legs over his shoulder and fastened his mouth over her clit.

Fire burst through her at the contact. She gasped, flattened her hands to the wall, tossed her head back, and groaned. "Cage…"

"Hmm." He didn't let her go, didn't come up for air, just continued to savor her as if she was the sweetest treat to ever cross his lips.

Under his mouth, she unraveled. It was so intimate, so passionate. He held nothing back, unabashedly pursuing her pleasure. Every touch demanded she give it to him. As his tongue laved her clit again and again, concentrating exactly where she needed him, Karis canted her hips to him, opened for him, gave him everything, including her mounting need.

She thrust her hands in his wavy hair and gave a tug. "Oh, god. Please…"

"Come for me," he muttered roughly against her thigh. "Cupcakes have cream frosting, and I want all your sweetness on my tongue."

Cage had a dirty mouth. She remembered that from New Year's Eve. Now, like then, his wicked words unwound her and left her breathless.

Under the lash of his tongue and the nip of his teeth, the burn behind her clit swelled and grew. She felt it filling her veins, flooding her head, drowning her in a well of ecstasy.

When he sucked her into his mouth again, she went under with a long, harsh cry. Cage only took that as his sign to go at her with more gusto, and he wrung out every moment of bliss from her body he could. He left her panting and limp and glowing.

He stood slowly, kissing his way up her body. When his face

filled her vision, he was wearing that proud, cocky grin. "Best cupcake ever."

Despite feeling completely spent, she laughed. "You certainly ate it with gusto."

"I have a feeling it will always be my favorite dessert." He dragged his lips up her neck. "In fact, I may never eat another cupcake again."

When he straightened and pressed his forehead against hers, he stared at her with a dark, dead-serious gaze. Something about it seized her insides. In the next instant, she knew why, and her breath caught.

Cage wasn't playing in any way—except for keeps.

"Are you going to take me to bed now?" Her voice shook.

"Absolutely," he murmured as he lifted her rubbery legs and settled them in the crook of his arm, supporting her back with the other. A few steps later, they were on the bed, Cage on top of her. Together, they pushed and tugged and yanked until he was naked. Well, she did more of the work. He seemed orally fixated on her mouth and her nipples…and she wasn't complaining a bit.

Finally, he fished a condom from his pants and rolled it down his length with one hand, opening her to the swollen crest he fitted against her entrance with the other. Karis held her breath, lifted her hips, aching with the wait to feel him deep. No one had ever given her pleasure like Cage Bryant. No man had left his mark on her heart the way this one had. Sure, she'd had silly fairy-tale dreams of meeting Mr. Wonderful…but that had been a fantasy borne of the broken promises of a father to his little girl, of her mother's endless string of terrible boyfriends.

Cage was real.

"Ready?"

"Hurry…" she moaned.

"Yeah. I'm going to lose my fucking mind without you, too.

DEVOTED TO WICKED

Hold on to me."

That was all the warning he gave her before he braced himself, spread her wider, and filled her with one rough thrust.

He delved deep. Her head fell back. Her nails dug in. Her breath rushed out in a moan. Already, he was everything she remembered and more.

"Oh, fuck," he groaned loud and low. "You feel so damn good, cupcake. Jesus…"

"Amazing." She couldn't quite catch her breath. She definitely couldn't stop wriggling under him. "I need more, Cage."

He breathed harshly against her skin. "I'll always need more from you."

Karis had no time to process his confession before he plunged into her again and again, establishing a hard, slow rhythm that scraped every nerve ending and held her in thrall. Every time he shoved inside her, he wrung a gasp, a whimper, or a kiss from her.

"Faster!"

"Not until I make you come," he gritted out between clenched teeth. "Once you're there…"

Couldn't he feel her tightening around him, clamping down on him? Her folds swelled. The need ratcheted up so hard and fast Karis found herself wrapping her arms and legs around him, pressing her lips across his bulging shoulder when she wasn't panting in his ear.

God, this need felt as if she hadn't had sex in four years instead of four weeks. She rocked under him, lifting and rolling with him, welcoming him deeper than ever. He gave more. Need gripped her. She was going under again. Holy hell, no man had ever driven her to two monumental orgasms in under ten minutes. A few had even spent hours trying to get one from her and left empty-handed. But Cage touched her in every way, even her heart. It swelled and beat and filled as he did the same to her

31

pussy.

As she sat on the precipice of orgasmic bliss, Karis sank her fingers into his shoulders and squeezed hard.

He read her signals. "Oh, cupcake… Yeah. Give it to me."

Then he pistoned into her faster. The ache grew to something that nearly engulfed her, gnawed at the last of her composure, and now threatened to swallow her whole. Her body pulsed and jolted as she cried his name, giving him every bit of her bliss.

And her heart.

Yes, she'd feared this man would steal her heart on New Year's Eve, but now it was official. She loved him. Actually loved him. She'd been infatuated with guys enough to know the difference. She'd seen her mother "fall" enough to know when it wasn't real.

Her heart told her this was love.

As if he felt it too, he groaned as he emptied inside her with short, sharp thrusts and buried his head in the crook of her neck. When he came up for air, he looked right into her eyes. "I love you."

She smiled at him. "I was…um, just thinking the same about you."

His grin overtook his whole face. "Were you now? You sure you don't need round two in order to know for sure?"

Karis loved the way he played in bed. She loved the way she felt cherished when she was with him. Heck, she loved everything about him.

She slapped on an answering smile. "You know, I just might…"

CAN A MAN *die of happiness?* That question circled Cage's brain as he lay beside Karis. She'd tangled her arms and legs up with his, resting her head on his arm. Her lashes swept dark half-moons over her cheeks. Absently, he brushed his fingers through her silky hair as she slept.

The two days of sex, sun, and talk they'd shared had been amazing. Idyllic. Exactly what he'd needed to be sure Karis was his future. They might be opposites, but they had a surprising amount in common. They wanted the same things out of life—marriage, family, happiness. She was still a little skittish, and he understood with her background. But he also wasn't giving up. Cage intended to leave here knowing Karis Weston was his.

What he didn't like was how quiet Miguel had gotten. Maybe the asswipe would just go away since Cage had made it clear the waiter couldn't fly under his radar anymore. But his gut told him Miguel wasn't a quitter. He was even more convinced after Trees called back to say that several past female hotel guests had registered complaints about the wannabe Romeo's forward behavior. And what do you know? Several had reported their passports stolen, too. No one had fired the little shit because the manager of the property, Raul Nabaté, was his uncle. And no one had caught Miguel red-handed.

Cage intended to change that.

With any luck, Karis's new passport would come in today so they could get out of here, go home, and start their future. He was still plotting the best attack plan—besides beating the devil out of the prick—when his cupcake stirred beside him.

"Morning." Karis stretched with a smile. "What should we do today? Yoga class starts at ten. Interested?"

Cage kissed her forehead. He already knew from inquiring that Miguel was due to report to work at the same time. That would be his best opportunity to resolve Karis's Latin-lover problem. If his hunch wasn't right, Cage would have another man-to-pipsqueak chat with Miguel after he filed a formal complaint with hotel management and hoped they did something this time. But he'd rather not leave anything to chance.

"Nope, but you go ahead. I'll check on your passport while you're downward dogging. If it's ready, I'll see about getting us some flights home. If not, we'll grab some beach time."

"Then a sultry siesta?" she suggested with a wink.

"Is there any other kind?"

Karis laughed, and he held her close as they dipped in for a quick shower…that turned into a deep, slow orgasm. Then they grabbed some breakfast from the buffet, and Cage started feeling her out on the subject of a deeper commitment. He was getting green-light vibes when she suddenly looked at her watch.

"Damn. I've got less than ten minutes until class starts. I need to go."

"I'll walk you there and meet you when it's finished."

She stood and kissed him slowly. "I'll thank you properly later."

"I'll definitely look forward to that."

As their embrace ended, he saw Miguel in his peripheral vision. The asshole hadn't missed their exchange. And since he was wearing his starched uniform, he must be on duty. Perfect.

After a glare Miguel's way, Cage escorted Karis to the yoga studio, then dashed through the lobby and exited the hotel, catching a taxi. He had just under an hour to dig up some answers.

Since Trees had hacked the resort's entire file on Miguel Nabaté, including his home address, Cage intended to make full use of the information. No, he wasn't playing by the rules…but neither was Miguel.

Hoping the guy lived alone, he exited the taxi in front of the old, blue-stucco apartment building. "Wait here."

When the driver nodded, Cage sought out apartment 201. It took less than two minutes to find the door, pick the lock, and begin sifting through the cluttered space. Cage thanked his police training. He'd searched hundreds of locations and had a nose for contraband. He'd find whatever Miguel had stashed here. Maybe he should feel bad about the illegal search and seizure. But he didn't—in the least.

What a fucking slob. Cage grimaced at the nasty pad just before he struck gold. Inside the drawer of a dresser, he found a half dozen passports, all reported stolen—including Karis's.

"Gotcha, you motherfucker."

Shoving them all in his pocket, Cage rearranged the apartment exactly as he'd found it, then locked the door behind him. A glance at his phone told him he had thirty minutes before Karis's yoga class ended. She would be safe with the others until then.

Jumping back into the taxi, Cage urged the driver to floor it to the hotel. Everything was going according to plan...

Until he returned to the resort's yoga studio and found Karis gone. With the class in session, he couldn't ask anyone questions.

Cursing, his heart pounding, Cage dashed to their room to see if she'd returned there. Empty. Nor could he find her in the gym, hanging around the lobby, or by the pool...

Don't panic. Don't panic. He repeated the litany over and over. It didn't help.

When he poked his head into the restaurant where Miguel worked, he couldn't find the creeper there, either. That made Cage's gut tighten with worry even more. When he stopped a pair of waitresses to ask around about Miguel, they shrugged, swearing they hadn't seen him in a while.

Son of a bitch. Raking a hand through his hair, Cage forced himself to think. Where would Miguel have taken her? He'd have many options, and the resort was too big to search quickly without help.

Hotel security. Cage sprinted to the guard station and found a strapping guy in a pseudo-police uniform, baton at his side, shiny shoes gracing his feet. His name tag proclaimed him Mateo. Yeah, this guy was mostly for show, but he had a gleam in his eyes like he was itching for real action.

Cage rolled the dice and hoped for the best. "One of your waiters, Miguel Nabaté, has a habit of stealing women's passports so he can strand them at the resort and seduce them. The guy took my girlfriend's passport a few days ago." He tossed the collection of official documents he'd collected at Miguel's apartment on the counter. "And now she's missing. I need help finding her ASAP. He's potentially dangerous."

The guard flipped quickly through all the passports and swore. Face tightening, he barked a few words of Spanish into the walkie-talkie sitting near his elbow. After a few static-filled replies, Mateo regarded Cage with fury.

"Mr. Nabaté has been warned repeatedly that his nephew is a liability. Everyone on property is looking for Miguel now. A scan of the employee parking lot indicates his car is still here. No one has seen him leave the property. Where did you last see your girlfriend?"

When Cage explained, Mateo called to speak with the yoga instructor. The exchange was brief, and when it ended, the guard nodded as he hung up. "Your girlfriend stayed for roughly half the class, then excused herself because she received an urgent note. The instructor did not know what it said. I will access the camera feed in the common areas to see if I can ascertain what happened next."

"Great. Can I help?" Cage flashed his Dallas PD badge.

Mateo was taken aback, but shrugged. "Of course."

After a quick troll through the security footage, they finally spotted Karis leaving the yoga studio. She paced down the hall, then passed through the lobby. She didn't glance twice at the elevators, but dashed through the double door outside, toward the ocean, looking frantic. She paused on the back patio and looked around, glancing at the note in her hand.

Miguel wandered into the shot a moment later, said something in her ear, and patted her on the back. Seconds after, she went limp in his arms. Then the dirtbag dragged her behind a bush and down a little-traveled path, out of the shot of the camera. The time and date stamp said that had happened twenty minutes ago.

Cage's heart stopped. He'd gone out of his way to reconnect with her after their New Year's fling. They'd cleared the air and gotten truly close. It couldn't be too late. "What's down that path?"

The guard shrugged. "A liquor storage shed for the bar."

"Take me there." It wasn't a request.

Mateo didn't hesitate. He bellowed into the walkie-talkie, then strapped it to his belt before leading the charge out the back of the resort.

The crashing waves of the ocean and the sound of his pounding heart were all Cage could hear—until they were mere feet from the shed. Then Karis's scream of terror split the air.

Breaking out in a cold sweat, Cage lunged for the door and tried to rip it off its hinges. Of course, the bastard had locked it.

"Get me in there," he growled at Mateo.

But the tall guard was already shoving the key into the lock and wrenching the door open. Cage shouldered the guy out of the way and found Karis trapped in the corner, holding the strap of her torn bikini with one hand and threatening Miguel with a hefty bottle of booze in the other.

Cage saw red. Karis was his. *No* other man would ever touch her, especially against her will.

Miguel whirled to the sound of the interruption with a snarl. Cage charged him and grabbed the waiter by the back of his stiff jacket, punching him in the jaw. "I warned you. Back away from my girlfriend."

"Cage!" Her voice trembled.

He wanted to go to her, comfort her. First, he had to deal with the threat.

"It was a simple misunderstanding," Miguel backpedaled. "She said she wanted a tour of the private areas. I misinterpreted her request and—"

"Fuck you. I found the passports you've stolen from other women in your apartment. Security knows. Your uncle soon will, too. You're going down. And you're not putting another finger on my woman—or any other—for a long while.

Miguel sputtered and blanched. "No. No, I—"

"Shut up, asshole." Karis swung the bottle and broke it over his head.

The scent of cheap gin doused Miguel as he crumpled to the ground.

It was over. Thank god.

"We apologize profusely, señorita," Mateo said as he motioned to his peers to take Miguel's inert form from the shed.

Karis looked away from the sight, flinging herself against Cage with teary eyes. "Thank you. The note said you were hurt and needed me."

"Miguel tricked you."

She nodded. "I feel so dumb. I didn't think. Thank you for coming after me…"

He cradled her face in his hands. "I always will. I love you, cupcake. You okay?"

"Yes." She hugged him, silently assuring him. "You got to me before…"

Cage knew all too well what Miguel had intended. He'd seen the angry lust in the man's eyes. He'd seen that same look in others he'd arrested, too. He held her as tightly as he dared, grateful she was safe in his arms.

"I'm so damn glad." He caressed her back with a soothing touch. "I found your passport. You want to go home?"

Obviously, there would be a security interview, police reports, and other official stuff first. But Cage was determined to get her on a plane tonight.

She nodded, tears spilling. "Yes."

"You got it. Would you…um, want to move in with me when we get there?" As soon as the words slipped out, Cage almost groaned aloud. Could his timing be any worse?

"Yes." The emphatic nod of her head backed up her answer.

He hesitated. Since everything between them was going surprisingly well, maybe he should go for broke. "How about if we got married, too? Maybe it's too fast but I know how I feel about you."

"Yes." Karis pressed a kiss to his lips.

The grin that crossed his face spread through his whole body. "Really? You want to marry me? You're not just saying yes on autopilot?"

An adoring smile creased her face. "I know what I feel, too. You're the love I've been looking for since I stopped believing in fairy tales. I'm not saying yes on autopilot. I really would love to be your wife."

"Well, all right! Let's go home, get a ring on your finger, and start our lives." He helped her attach her torn strap, then took her hand in his and led her outside.

They emerged into the waiting crowd of security. The police

took Miguel away, and his uncle frowned fiercely, shaking his head.

Once the red tape was behind them and they were waiting at the gate for their flight home, Cage kissed her softly. "Hey, fiancée. I love you."

She cupped his cheek, looking deep into his eyes. "You've made the dreams I stopped believing in come true. I love you, too."

Cage knew he'd never get tired of the view. "And just think, all the cupcake I want for the rest of my life. Hmm. I'm hungry right now…"

Karis laughed as they boarded the plane to start their perfect future.

Read on for excerpts and more by Shayla Black!

DEVOTED TO PLEASURE

Devoted Lovers, Book 1
By Shayla Black
NOW AVAILABLE!

Bodyguard and former military man Cutter Bryant has always done his duty—no matter what the personal cost. Now he's taking one last high-octane, high-dollar assignment before settling down in a new role that means sacrificing his chance at love. But he never expects to share an irresistible chemistry with his beautiful new client.

Fame claimed Shealyn West suddenly and with a vengeance after starring in a steamy television drama, but it has come at the expense of her heart. Though she's pretending to date a co-star for her image, a past mistake has come back to haunt her. With a blackmailer watching her every move and the threat of career-ending exposure looming, Shealyn hires Cutter to shore up her security, never imagining their attraction will be too powerful to contain.

As Shealyn and Cutter navigate the scintillating line between business and pleasure, they unravel a web of secrets that threaten their relationship and their lives. When danger strikes, Cutter must decide whether to follow his heart for the first time, or risk losing Shealyn forever.

EXCERPT

"CUTTER?"

She sounded unsure. Was she afraid of the dark? Of what had happened with her blackmailer earlier? Or what might happen between the two of them next?

He moved closer slowly, giving her plenty of time to back away. "I'm here."

Shealyn allayed his worries when, instead of retreating or flipping the light switch beside her, she reached for him, fingers curling around his arm like she was grabbing a lifeline.

Cutter edged into her personal space. She didn't put distance between them, just exhaled in relief and pressed herself against him.

Oh, god. She wanted something from him that didn't feel merely like comfort.

He was going to have to deal with the two dirtbags who were after Shealyn and convince her to let him hunt them down to see justice served. To do that, he would have to focus on something besides her sweet, addicting mouth.

But unless someone charged in, gun drawn, threats spewing, that wasn't happening now.

The thought that she was here, safe, and wanting his touch tore the leash from his restraint.

Cutter took her shoulders in hand and nudged her back against the wall. She went with a gasp. In one motion, he flattened himself against her, palms braced above her head, hips rocking against the soft pad of her pussy. He couldn't hold in the groan that tore from his chest.

"I shouldn't do this but . . . goddamn it. If you don't want this, stop me. A word will do it." Cutter tried to wait for her assent, but the sensual curve of her throat beckoned him. He bent, inhaled her, grew dizzy from her scent. It reminded him of the gardenias Mama used to grow in the spring. Blended with that scent was the thick aroma of her arousal, pungent and dizzying. "Say it now, sweetheart."

Shealyn ignored him, rocking against him, her head falling to the side as she offered him her neck—and any other part of her he wanted. "Why would I tell you to go when I want you closer?"

She wasn't going to stop him. And she wouldn't save him from himself. Drowning in her would be a singular pleasure that would be worth whatever the price—even his heart.

Cutter fastened his mouth to hers again and tugged on the bottom of her turtleneck, only breaking the kiss when the sweater came between them. The moment he yanked it over her head and tossed it to the floor, he captured her lips once more, growling at the heady feel of the warm, smooth skin of her back, bare under his palms.

Shealyn moved restlessly against him, fisting his T-shirt in her hands and giving it a tug. She raised the thin cotton over his abdomen and chest, but got stuck at his shoulders. Her moan pleaded with him. She wanted the shirt gone and she wanted it now.

Cutter took over, tearing his mouth from hers and shrugging off the holster. When it fell to the tile with a seemingly distant clang, he reached behind his neck and jerked the T-shirt from his body. Using one hand, he tossed it aside. The other slid down Shealyn's spine to cup her pretty, pert ass.

Jesus, she was like all his hottest fantasies, but better. Because she was real and, right now, she desired him.

When his second hand joined the first on her luscious backside, he bent and lifted her, parting her legs and sliding between them with a growl. She wrapped her legs around him, clutched his shoulders, and swayed against him as if she wanted nothing more than to be as close as two people could.

The attraction between them was chemical, animal—unlike anything he'd ever felt. He needed to get on top of her, be inside of her, root as deep into her as he could. The wall had been convenient for a mere kiss, but it was a damn hindrance now. He couldn't have Shealyn the way he craved her here.

"Hold on to me," he demanded as he clasped her tighter and trekked down the hall, across the expansive living room and the glitzy view, then strode into her bedroom.

The stars of L.A. beckoned beyond the French doors. He didn't give them a second glance, not when he had Shealyn West in his arms.

She pressed kisses to his jaw, his lips, his forehead. She nipped at his earlobe, her soft pant a shiver down his spine. "Cutter . . . I-I need you."

Yeah, he understood her perfectly, even though nothing between them made a damn lick of sense. But tonight had flipped some switch inside him. He could no longer pretend—to her or himself—that his feelings for her were strictly professional. No, he craved her alive and responding, clawing, wailing, begging, seemingly his . . . even if it wouldn't last.

"I'm here." He laid her across the bed and climbed over her, settling his hips between her legs. He wished they were naked. He wished he was inside of her, already one with her as he pressed his erection to her softness. "I'm not going anywhere unless you want me to."

She paused and blinked up at him as if she was trying to gauge how much he really meant that. Why would she doubt him? Or her own appeal, given how quickly she'd dismantled his self-control?

"I don't want you anywhere else." She skated her palms over his shoulders, even as she parted her thighs to take him deeper.

Her touch sent an electric reaction zipping through his veins. He curled his fingers around one of her shoulders in return, lowering her bra strap. When she didn't object, he tugged down the lacy cup and exposed her breast.

Holy hell. He had to have that taut pink flesh in his mouth now. He had to savor her, suck her like a sweet summer berry. He craved his lips against her skin.

Without another thought, he lowered his head and lapped her rigid peak with his tongue. She gasped, arched up, clasping him like she never wanted him to let go. He sucked harder.

He'd known she would be beautiful. He'd known she would feel like heaven. He had never expected her to respond so perfectly to him, with little catches of breath as she burrowed her fingers in his hair, urging him closer.

Under his body, Shealyn writhed, trying to shimmy out of her bra. She couldn't reach the clasp—and he couldn't bring himself to allow enough space between them for her to do the job—but she still managed to work the other strap down and peel the cup away.

Cutter seized the unclaimed space instantly. He broke the suction from the first peak and shifted to the other. Oh, hell yes. Soft and velvety, her breasts beckoned him the way the rest of her did—every part from her pouty lips to her sweetly sassy spirit. He loved that she wasn't all bones, hadn't subscribed to the Hollywood belief that a woman with hips should immediately begin starving to save her career.

He couldn't wait to see Shealyn naked, wrap his arms around her, sink into her. Take her. Make her his for the few golden hours it lasted.

With a move Cage had taught him in high school, Cutter slid a hand beneath her and pinched the clasp of her bra. The undergarment propped free, and he stripped it from her body.

A voice in the back of his head reminded him that getting inside her shouldn't be his top priority. But a primal fever burned him, urging him on. It wouldn't cool and it wouldn't bow to logic or civility. It didn't give a shit right now if he was professional. It could care less what else was going on in their lives. It wanted to claim Shealyn, mark her as his woman.

MORE THAN WANT YOU

More Than Words, Book 1
By Shayla Black
NOW AVAILABLE!

I'm Maxon Reed—real estate mogul, shark, asshole. If a deal isn't high profile and big money, I pass. Now that I've found the property of a lifetime, I'm jumping. But one tenacious bastard stands between me and success—my brother. I'll need one hell of a devious ploy to distract cynical Griff. Then fate drops a luscious redhead in my lap who's just his type.

Sassy college senior Keeley Kent accepts my challenge to learn how to become Griff's perfect girlfriend. But somewhere between the makeover and the witty conversation, I'm having trouble resisting her. The quirky dreamer is everything I usually don't tolerate. But she's beyond charming. I more than want her; I'm desperate to own her. I'm not even sure how drastic I'm willing to get to make her mine—but I'm about to find out.

EXCERPT

"THIS WILL BE our last song for the set. If you have requests, write them down and leave them in the jar." She points to the clear vessel at her feet. "We'll be back to play in thirty. If you have a dirty proposition, I'll entertain them at the bar in five." She says the words like she's kidding.

I, however, am totally serious.

Keeley starts her next song, a more recent pop tune, in a breathy, a capella murmur. "Can't keep my hands to myself."

She taps her thigh in a rhythm only she can hear until the band joins during the crescendo to the chorus. Keeley bounces her way through the lyrics with a flirty smile. It's both alluring and fun, a tease of a song.

Though I rarely smile, I find myself grinning along.

As she finishes, I glance around. There's more than one hungry dog with a bone in this damn bar.

I didn't get ahead in business or life by being polite or waiting my turn. She hasn't even wrapped her vocal cords around the last note but I'm on my feet and charging across the room.

I'm the first one to reach the corner of the bar closest to the stage. I prop my elbow on the slightly sticky wood to claim my territory, then glare back at the three other men who think they should end Keeley's supposed sex drought. They are not watering her garden, and my snarl makes that clear.

One sees my face, stops in his tracks, and immediately backs off. Smart man.

Number Two looks like a smarmy car salesman. He rakes Keeley up and down with his gaze like she's a slab of beef, but she's flirting my way as she tucks her mic on its stand. I smile back.

She's not really my type, but man, I'd love to hit that.

Out of the corner of my eye, I watch the approaching dirtbag finger his porn 'stouche. To stake my claim, I reach out to help Keeley off the stage. She looks pleasantly surprised by my gesture as she wraps her fingers around mine.

I can be a gentleman...when it suits me.

Fuck, she's warm and velvety, and her touch makes my cock jolt. Her second would-be one-night stand curses then slinks back to his seat.

That leaves me to fend off Number Three. He looks like a WWE reject—hulking and hit in the face too many times. If she prefers brawn over brains, I'll have to find another D-cup distraction for Griff.

That would truly suck. My gut tells me Keeley is perfect for the job.

Would it be really awful if I slept with her before I introduced her to my brother?

MORE THAN NEED YOU

More Than Words, Book 2
By Shayla Black
NOW AVAILABLE!

I'm Griffin Reed—cutthroat entrepreneur and competitive bastard. Trust is a four-letter word and everyone is disposable...except Britta Stone. Three years ago, she was my everything before I stupidly threw her away. I thought I'd paid for my sin in misery—until I learned we have a son. Finding out she's engaged to a bore who's rushing her to the altar pisses me off even more. I intend to win her back so we can raise our boy together. I'll have to get ruthless, of course. Luckily, that's one of my more singular talents.

Sixty days. That's what I'm asking the gritty, independent single mother to give me—twenty-four/seven. Under my roof. And if I have my way, in my bed. Britta says she wants nothing to do with me. But her body language and passionate kisses make her a liar. Now all I have to do is coax her into surrendering to the old magic between us. Once I have her right where I want her, I'll do whatever it takes to prove I more than need her.

MORE THAN LOVE YOU

More Than Words, Book 3
By Shayla Black
NOW AVAILABLE!

I'm Noah Weston. For a decade, I've quarterbacked America's most iconic football team and plowed my way through women. Now I'm transitioning from star player to retired jock—with a cloud of allegation hanging over my head. So I'm escaping to the private ocean-front paradise I bought for peace and quiet. What I get instead is stubborn, snarky, wild, lights-my-blood-on-fire Harlow Reed. Since she just left a relationship in a hugely viral way, she should be the last woman I'm seen with.

On second thought, we can help each other...

I need a steady, supportive "girlfriend" for the court of public opinion, not entanglements. Harlow is merely looking for nonstop sweaty sex and screaming orgasms that wring pleasure from her oh-so-luscious body. Three months—that's how long it should take for us both to scratch this itch and leave our respective scandals behind. But the more I know this woman, the less I can picture my life without her. And when I'm forced to choose, I realize I don't merely want her in my bed or need her for a ruse. I more than love her enough to do whatever it takes to make her mine for good.

MORE THAN CRAVE YOU

More Than Words, Book 4
By Shayla Black
Coming September 18, 2018!

I'm Evan Cook—billionaire tech entrepreneur and widower. Professionally, I've got it all. But since my wife died, my personal life has fallen apart. Remarrying seems like the obvious answer, so I place an ad. I'm not asking for much. The ideal woman only needs to be smart, organized, pretty, and helpful—both in and out of bed—without expecting romance. I never thought to look right in front of me...but it turns out that Nia Wright, my sexy, sassy assistant, just might be the perfect candidate.

After an unexpectedly hot night together, I'm ready to stop interviewing strangers and simply marry her. On paper, she ticks every box on my list. Best of all, she's far too sensible to fall for me. I didn't see the flaw in my logic until it was too late. I never thought I'd lose my heart for the first time. And I definitely never imagined Nia could consume me. But she's harboring a secret that could tear us apart. Can I prove I more than crave her before it's too late?

ABOUT SHAYLA BLACK

Shayla Black is the *New York Times* and *USA Today* bestselling author of more than sixty novels. For twenty years, she's written contemporary, erotic, paranormal, and historical romances via traditional, independent, foreign, and audio publishers. Her books have sold millions of copies and been published in a dozen languages.

Raised an only child, Shayla occupied herself with lots of daydreaming, much to the chagrin of her teachers. In college, she found her love for reading and realized that she could have a career publishing the stories spinning in her imagination. Though she graduated with a degree in Marketing/Advertising and embarked on a stint in corporate America to pay the bills, her heart has always been with her characters. She's thrilled that she's been living her dream as a full-time author for the past eight years.

Shayla currently lives in North Texas with her wonderfully supportive husband, her daughter, and two spoiled tabbies. In her "free" time, she enjoys reality TV, reading, and listening to an eclectic blend of music.

Connect with me online:
Website: shaylablack.com
VIP Reader Newsletter: shayla.link/nwsltr
Facebook Author Page: facebook.com/ShaylaBlackAuthor
Facebook Book Beauties Chat Group: shayla.link/FBChat
Instagram: instagram.com/ShaylaBlack
Book+Main Bites: bookandmainbites.com/users/62
Twitter: twitter.com/Shayla_Black

Google +: shayla.link/googleplus
Amazon Author: shayla.link/AmazonFollow
BookBub: shayla.link/BookBub
Goodreads: shayla.link/goodreads
YouTube: shayla.link/youtube

If you enjoyed this book, please review it or recommend it to others so they can find it, too.

Keep in touch by engaging with me through one of the links above. Subscribe to my VIP Readers newsletter for exclusive excerpts and hang out in my Facebook Book Beauties group for live weekly video chats. I love talking to readers!

OTHER BOOKS BY SHAYLA BLACK

CONTEMPORARY ROMANCE

MORE THAN WORDS

More Than Want You
More Than Need You
More Than Love You

Coming Soon:
More Than Crave You (September 18, 2018)

THE WICKED LOVERS (COMPLETE SERIES)

Wicked Ties
Decadent
Delicious
Surrender to Me
Belong to Me
"Wicked to Love" (novella)
Mine to Hold
"Wicked All the Way" (novella)
Ours to Love
"Wicked All Night" (Wicked And Dangerous Anthology)
"Forever Wicked" (novella)
Theirs to Cherish
His to Take
"Pure Wicked" (novella)
Wicked for You
Falling in Deeper
"Dirty Wicked" (novella)
"A Very Wicked Christmas" (short)
Holding on Tighter

THE DEVOTED LOVERS
Devoted to Pleasure

"Devoted to Wicked" (novella)

Coming Soon:
Devoted to Love (July 2, 2019)

SEXY CAPERS

Bound And Determined
Strip Search
"Arresting Desire" (Hot In Handcuffs Anthology)

THE PERFECT GENTLEMEN (by Shayla Black and Lexi Blake)

Scandal Never Sleeps
Seduction in Session
Big Easy Temptation
Smoke and Sin

Coming Soon:
At the Pleasure of the President (Fall 2018)

MASTERS OF MÉNAGE (by Shayla Black and Lexi Blake)

Their Virgin Captive
Their Virgin's Secret
Their Virgin Concubine
Their Virgin Princess
Their Virgin Hostage
Their Virgin Secretary
Their Virgin Mistress

Coming Soon:
Their Virgin Bride (TBD)

DOMS OF HER LIFE (by Shayla Black, Jenna Jacob, and Isabella LaPearl)
Raine Falling Collection (Complete Series)

One Dom To Love
The Young And The Submissive
The Bold and The Dominant
The Edge of Dominance

Heavenly Rising Collection
The Choice

Coming Soon:
The Chase (2019)

THE MISADVENTURES SERIES

Misadventures of a Backup Bride

Coming Soon:
Misadventures with My Ex (December 25, 2018)

STANDALONE TITLES

Naughty Little Secret
Watch Me
Dangerous Boys And Their Toy
"Her Fantasy Men" (Four Play Anthology)
A Perfect Match
His Undeniable Secret (Sexy Short)

HISTORICAL ROMANCE (as Shelley Bradley)

The Lady And The Dragon
One Wicked Night
Strictly Seduction
Strictly Forbidden

BROTHERS IN ARMS MEDIEVAL TRILOGY

His Lady Bride (Book 1)
His Stolen Bride (Book 2)
His Rebel Bride (Book 3)

PARANORMAL ROMANCE

THE DOOMSDAY BRETHREN

Tempt Me With Darkness
"Fated" (e-novella)
Seduce Me In Shadow
Possess Me At Midnight
"Mated" – Haunted By Your Touch Anthology
Entice Me At Twilight
Embrace Me At Dawn

Join the

ShaylaBLACK

Book Beauties
Facebook Group
http://shayla.link/FBChat

Join me for live,
interactive video chats
every #WineWednesday.
Be there for breaking
Shayla news, fun,
positive community,
giveaways, and more!

VIP Readers
NEWSLETTER
at ShaylaBlack.com

Be among the first to get
your greedy hands on
Shayla Black news, juicy
excerpts, cool VIP
giveaways—and more!

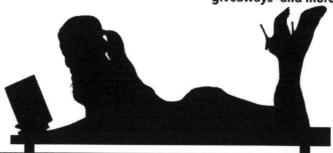

41355303R00035

Made in the USA
San Bernardino, CA
02 July 2019